Comedy Around Cowboys

Stu Campbell

With Illustrations by R. Loren Schmidt

This is a work of fiction.

ISBN: 978-0-9962019-9-5

6 5 4 3

Edited by Mira Perrizo
Cover and text design by D.K. Luraas
Cover and interior illustrations by R. Loren Schmidt
Author photo by Elizabeth Dobbs

Printed in the United States of America

Contents

In the Wrong Position?

When I was a kid, only sixteen, I got a job working on Jim Murphy's Ox Yoke Ranch, outside Emigrant, Montana, and north of Yellowstone National Park. A school friend of mine, Dick, had worked up there the previous summer and had gotten me the job.

The Ox Yoke was a dude and cattle ranch. Jim had a few cows and he let the dudes help move the cattle. I hadn't had any experience around dudes, and Dick pumped me full of information about the dude business. I'd had plenty of experience around cattle and horses, plenty for a sixteen-year-old kid and figured I was a pretty fair hand.

I showed up at Jim's a day after school was out and got settled in the bunkhouse. I was the only help, other than the maids. They had their own sleeping quarters. During supper that night, Jim outlined my duties.

I was to get up early, light the stoves in each one of the cabins, clean out the flues in the water heater, then saddle Banner, the jingle horse, and gather the horses. After that was done, we'd saddle the horses that we were going to use that day and commence to take the dudes riding. Jim would come with me in the morning, to give me an idea of how the horse pasture was laid out, after that I would be on my own.

Banner would be turned out into a small pasture and wouldn't be used again until the next day. His only job was to be the jingle horse.

The horse pasture was north of the barn and corrals, up on a big bluff. On top, the horses had plenty of room and the feed was good.

Jim had a pretty good string of horses for a dude outfit. They weren't head to tail horses and they could be ridden just about anywhere. During the summer, I had the opportunity to ride just about all of them. I don't remember all their names, it's been too many years ago, but I do remember a few of them.

Banner, of course, I remember. I rode him every morning all summer long gathering the horses. There was another horse I remember, Shaver, a good-looking sorrel horse with a light-colored mane and tail. Shaver was the favorite horse of a girl from back East who spent all summer at the ranch.

I also remember a gray two-year-old colt that I started during the summer, although I don't remember her name. I know she was ranch raised and wasn't too difficult to start.

I also remember a black and white paint mare—she was built a little different, kind of peaked in the rump. Her withers were almost nonexistent, kinda like a mule.

I only rode this horse once, because she was a favorite with the dudes. They thought she was pretty. But the time I rode her, we almost had disastrous results.

I had bought a new breast collar. Actually it was used, but it was new to me. When a young feller is just starting out, assembling his gear, quite often, because of the cost, he has to start with previously owned equipment; used. Such was my case. My equipment was old and used, but strong and serviceable.

I put my saddle on this black and white mare one morning. I normally don't tighten the cinch real tight, unless I'm going to do some heavy roping, and I didn't expect to do any on this day.

I mounted up and followed Jim to where we were going to

move some cows. The country was fairly steep, but we followed the trails and made it easier on the horses.

As we started down a particularly steep part of the trail, I felt my saddle slipping forward and the horse took a jump sideways.

"Whoa," I hollered.

Jim stopped his horse and turned around. By the time I got off, my saddle had slipped halfway down the horse's neck. I thought my cinch had busted. I was kind of clumsy getting off on that steep hill and almost fell down, but managed to hold onto the horse.

The cinch wasn't busted, just loose. As I reset my saddle, Jim said to me grinning, "Looks like to me you ought to use that breast collar on the other end!"

I didn't have a comment, but tightened my cinch tighter than it needed to be. I didn't want to entertain any ideas about my new breast collar, which I was quite proud of, being used as a britchen. I wasn't a mule man!

An Unscheduled Leave of Absence

My boss, Dave, had a good-looking gray horse. The horse was really built well, "structurally correct," in Dave's words. The horse was built good enough that a feller would do well if he entered him in halter-horse classes in the Quarter Horse shows. I admired this horse mostly because of the way he was built and because he had good ground manners. A feller could walk up to him and catch him anywhere.

Dave had bought the horse in Montana. He had built a pretty fair horse-trading business in Phoenix, Arizona, during the winter. He spent the summer in Colorado, outside of Estes Park.

Dave would buy these horses in Colorado, Wyoming, and Montana, do some riding on them, and then take them to Arizona. He'd do some more riding in Arizona and then offer them for sale. A lot of the horses he bought were reining-horse prospects and he was into the reining-horse contests fairly heavy.

One day Dave took the horse out and returned on foot, leading the horse. I saw him walking around the far end of the corral, the horse following placidly behind.

"What happened? Did the horse buck you off?" I was halfway teasing Dave; both of us were too old to be riding bucking horses.

"No," answered Dave. "I was in the middle of the river and I broke a rein. The horse got a little nervous and I rode to the bank and got off."

I looked him over. He didn't have any dust on him and his clothes were dry. He changed bridles, got on his horse, and resumed his ride. Nothing else happened for a couple of weeks.

Then Dave got the gray again and went for a ride. This time the gray returned without Dave and without the saddle! We immediately launched a search for Dave and the saddle. Somebody found Dave walking back to the barn, battered and bruised—walking with a limp and in obvious pain.

Somebody else found the saddle. It was not in such good shape. The rigging had been torn loose, the cinch busted, and it had a lot of scratches on it. The horse had probably got it caught on a pinyon tree and fought until something came loose, and it was busted up real good.

The cook insisted on taking Dave to the doctor and he went without an argument.

When they returned, everyone was interested in Dave's condition. He moved a little slowly and stiffly. He was a little unsteady going up the stairs into the house and once I thought I would have to catch him and keep him from falling backward. I was curious to know what happened, but as he wasn't feeling too hot, I declined to ask.

I asked the cook, "What's the situation?"

"Some bruised ribs and maybe a pulled muscle or two. According to the doctor, he'll need to take it easy for a few days."

Dave rested for a few days, mostly at my insistence. But he did come down to the office to monitor the selling of the horseback rides. We were taking tourists out on two- and four-hour horseback rides in Rocky Mountain National Park, and it was the busy part of the season.

When we had some free time, I asked him, "What happened between you and the gray?"

"The horse got scared, I don't know what scared him, maybe an elk. But he took the bit in his teeth and ran off. He's too strong for me to stop him. He's a strong horse! He brushed me off on a tree and there's where I got hurt. I haven't looked at my saddle yet, I was told it was torn up pretty bad."

I took him to where his saddle was and he inspected the damage. "I know a good saddle maker in Loveland that can fix it. I imagine it will cost plenty."

"What are you goin' to do with the gray?"

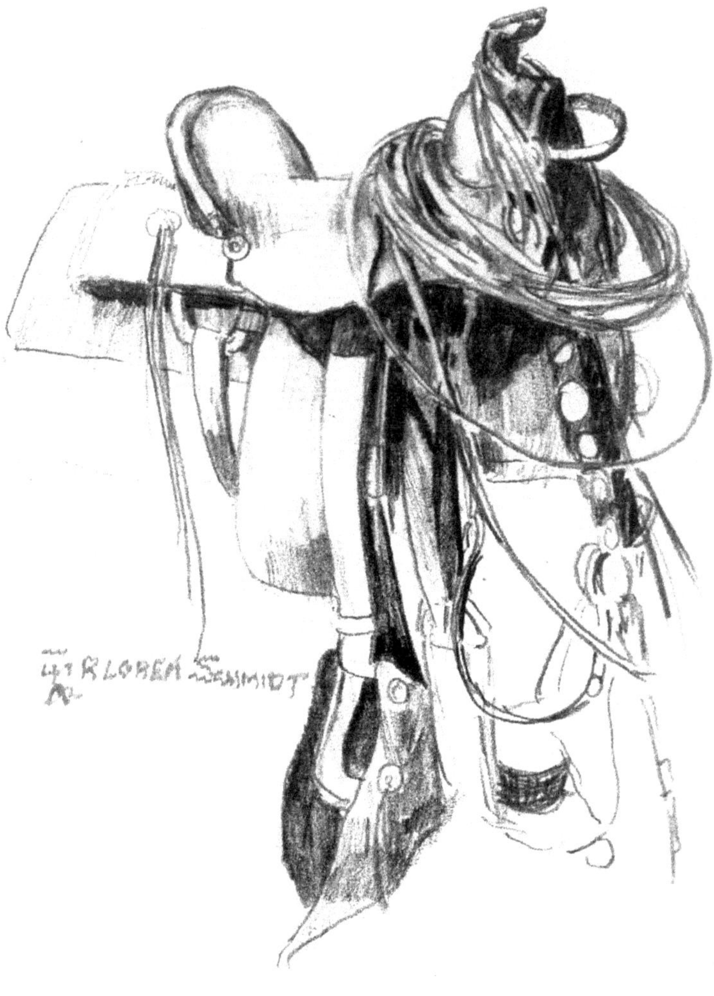

"I'll sell him. He's too much horse for my clients in Phoenix. He's a real cowboy's horse, he's no kid's horse."

"A lot of ridin' will help him as much as anything," I said.

"I don't know," said Dave. "The horse has a lot of fear and when he gets scared, he just runs off. When he goes, you can't stop him. It's the fight or flight response, only he appears to always take the flight option."

Dave took the horse to the next sale and I guessed he lost money on him when he sold him. I didn't ask him what the horse brought, I always thought that to be a breach of personal manners.

But Dave did assure me that the man that bought the horse knew exactly what he was getting.

"I told the man the whole history on the horse since I've had him," Dave told me. "I told him what I knew of his history before I got him and what he did to me and my saddle! He knew the whole story."

Getting Along Good

Like people, horses all have different personalities. And like people, each personality has to be handled differently. Most all of a horse's personality problems can be attributed to a person.

I don't really know why some horses are "pull backs" and I can't figure out why some horses develop that particular bad habit. I don't know how a person causes this bad habit unless initially the horse is tied too short, or somebody spooks the horse while he's tied.

A "pull back" is a horse that can't be tied to a hitch rail or a fence. For some reason or other, once they find out they're tied, they'll pull back, trying to free themselves and they won't stop until something breaks and they are free. It's an annoying, and to me, a disgusting habit, although I've owned a number of pull back horses. They were horses I bought at various horse sales and really knew nothing of their habits. I haven't tried to correct this bad habit; I figured the cost of replacing busted equipment wasn't worth the effort. Quite often the horse will stand if the lead rope is just wrapped around the hitch rail rather than being tied hard and fast.

A little bit of patience is required when dealing with pull back horses and quite often a lot of time is spent in catching the horse when he gets loose and putting him back where he belongs.

Another horse problem is a cinch-bound horse. A cinch-bound horse is a horse that will blow up or pull back when first saddled in the morning. I think this comes from tightening up a cinch too tight or jerking on the latigos when saddling, and is definitely caused by humans. I suppose it's sorta like having your belt or girdle too tight. I imagine it's quite uncomfortable. It can be a dangerous situation. Quite often the horse will rear up and fall over backward. This can be dangerous to the person saddling the horse and also result in a broken saddle tree.

I've owned a number of cinch-bound horses and worked on a lot of outfits that had cinch-bound horses. A number of times when working on a new outfit, the cow boss or foreman will say, "He's cinchy," and I have been alerted to the horse's particular problem.

I use a lot of care when saddling a strange horse for the first or second time. I don't tighten the cinch completely and never jerk on it. I just get the cinch a little snug and then walk the horse around a little, just enough so the horse knows it's there, then tighten the cinch.

In dealing with cinchy horses, a particular horse comes to mind. He was a buckskin and I sorta liked the way he was built. He was gentle and had the makings of being a good dude horse. He had been purchased at a horse sale by the owner of the dude outfit I worked on. Someone else fitted him to a saddle and when they pulled the cinch, the horse came over backward.

"I was told that horse was cinchy," said the boss. "I forgot to tell you."

The new hand that saddled the horse asked, "What's cinchy?" He wasn't only a new hand, he was also pretty green.

The situation was explained to him and he saddled the horse again the next day. Again the horse blew up.

The next day, to save time and trouble, I saddled the horse and didn't have a problem. I saddled the horse every day from

then until the end of the tourist season and didn't have any problems. I never tied the horse hard and fast, just wrapped the lead rope loosely around the hitch rail. I'd saddle the horse and walk him toward the barn twenty feet or so then pull the cinch tight enough to keep the saddle in place until the horse was to be used. The buckskin turned out to be a good dude horse, mostly carrying ladies around.

I worked for the same outfit for about four years and the buckskin was there for three of them. I never did have any problem with the horse, although he did pull back a few times. When newly hired hands went to saddle the horse, the boss would say,

"Let Stu saddle that horse. He gets along good with him."

Courage

A friend of my son's, Doug, wanted to be a bareback bronc rider. He was big and strong, but almost too big to ride broncs. But that was his desire.

I would go to the local rodeo every Saturday night, mostly to watch my son, Will, ride bulls. Will wanted to be a bull rider. He was getting entered each week in the bull riding, but he wasn't making it to the whistle very often. I couldn't tell if he was getting any better.

But, watching Doug each week, I could tell he wasn't getting any better. He was hitting the ground on a regular basis and it seemed like he was hitting the ground harder each week. Occasionally, he would get hurt, not really seriously, but he'd get up, holding a shoulder or walking back to the chutes limping.

Doug and his brother were good ropers and would get entered in the team roping every week and quite often they could come home with some money. I don't think Doug ever made enough money from team roping to cover what he lost trying to ride bareback broncs.

I've had a little experience riding bareback broncs, I did some of that when I was younger. Doug came to me and asked, "What can I do to start making some money on those bareback broncs?"

My answer was simple: "Stay on 'em 'till the whistle blows."

Flight Check

"I know that," said Doug, grinning. "But I'm doing something wrong. What is it?"

"Well Doug," I said, "you're too big to be ridin' those bareback broncs. They're generally smaller horses. They're usually faster an' quicker. Your reflexes aren't fast enough to stay with 'em. You can't adjust to their movement's quick enough. Consequently you're hittin' the ground. I'll bet it's starting to hurt, ain't it?"

"Yeah, but it's a lot of fun."

"Hittin' the ground is fun? It can't be much fun, hittin' the ground like that. I'd suggest you give up riding broncs. Stay with the team roping, you're a good roper an' you can rate cattle. You'll win more money, and you'll only be on the ground when you want to be."

Reluctantly, Doug gave up trying to ride bareback broncs.

It was sometime later when he came up to me while I was visiting with Will. "You know," he said, "you were the only one that had the courage to tell me exactly what you thought. And you were right."

"Doug," I said, "it doesn't take much courage to tell the truth. I simply told you the way I saw it. The truth never hurt me much, only when I got aside from it."

Punishment

The new hand was certainly enthusiastic and willing. I don't want to mention his name, he might see this, so I'll call him Roger. I thought he was also fairly immature for an eighteen-year-old. I was kinda dubious when I hired him, but we needed the help. I thought I could teach him what he needed to know to do what was needed. He didn't have much cowboy or horsemanship skills, but he was certainly willing. He did everything we asked him to do with a great deal of enthusiasm, although his enthusiasm caused him to have to go back and redo his efforts. Often, he would go off and start a particular project before I had the opportunity to tell him completely what I wanted him to do or how I wanted it done. That's what caused him to have to repeat his efforts. But he did it willingly. He also had plenty of energy.

We had a horse we called Rang because he was a mustang. I was told he was a kid's horse, gentle for any twelve- or thirteen-year-old. The horse was misrepresented to me, a common occurrence among horse traders. I had my suspicions about the horse when I bought him, but I figured we'd ride him for a few days before we rented him out, just to see what we had. If he didn't work out in the dude string, we could always use him as a guide horse.

After watching Roger ride for an hour, I decided to have him use Rang as a guide horse. I thought the horse could teach him more in a shorter period of time than I could with all the time in the world. I didn't have much time for teaching. I had to supervise a crew of about ten hands, size up tourists and assign their horses and run the office in addition to making sure our hands took care of about a hundred head of horses. I didn't have much time for teaching and Rang had plenty of time. He could teach while he was earning his room and board.

Rang was gentle enough. He just had plenty of energy—a little too much for the average dude to handle in the dude string. I thought they might make a good match. Both had a lot of energy and enthusiasm. And they seemed to get along good after a few days of riding.

When I assigned Rang to Roger, I told him, "This will be your horse while you're workin' here. You'll be responsible for him. You'll need to make sure he doesn't get any saddle sores, doesn't throw a shoe, and is generally all right to use every day. You treat him like you owned him."

"Yes sir!" was Roger's reply. "I'll do it!"

A few weeks went by and Roger and Rang seemed to be getting along well. Everyone stayed busy guiding horse rides for tourists and taking out breakfast and steak dinner rides. We had a steak ride just about every night and the crew really looked forward to those nights when we didn't have supper rides. I think they were getting tired of steak! But, when we didn't have a steak ride, they did get a chance to get done with work before dark.

One night we didn't have a steak ride. After our last hour ride went out, I had the crews start unsaddling horses. We'd get done a little earlier on this day.

Roger didn't go out on the last ride of the day and everyone welcomed his energy and enthusiasm when we were unsaddling. It wasn't long before we were done and we had some free time before the last ride of the day got back. We took care of the feeding and waited. I had plenty of paperwork to do and was busy in the office when they got in.

"The ride's back!" someone hollered.

"Unsaddle 'em an' we're done," I answered. "I've got some stuff to finish in here."

We waited until the horses finished their grain, took off the nose bags, turned them loose and started to head to the house. With his usual enthusiasm, Roger was one of the first to get into a car and leave. But I wasn't far behind him in the truck.

The next morning, I was the first to arrive at the corrals. The first thing I noticed was Rang tied to a tree outside the corral. Roger tied the horse outside the corral when he got off a ride so he could help the dudes get off their horses. Rang was saddled.

That's strange, I thought.

I left the horse tied where he was. When Roger arrived, I called him in the office.

"Is your horse okay today?" I asked.

"Yes," came the reply. "He was all right yesterday."

"He's still got plenty of energy and enthusiasm?" I asked.

"It seems like it," answered Roger.

"Does he have enough energy to work today?" I asked.

"Sure. Why are you asking me all this?"

"Look over there," I said pointing to the tree where Rang was tied.

Roger looked in the direction I pointed and his jaw dropped when he saw Rang.

"You left that horse tied to that tree all night, still saddled and with the bit still in his mouth, without feed or water," I said. "I'm not real happy about that and don't know what to do about it. I could make you go without a meal or two, but that might be considered cruel and unusual punishment. I'd like to tie you to a tree and leave you out all night, but I can't do that either. What do you suggest I do?"

"I'm really sorry," said Roger. "I don't know what to do."

"I'll tell you what to do. Right now, you unsaddle that horse and turn him loose in the corral. He's got the day off an' maybe tomorrow. I'll figure out what to do with you later. But anybody that would treat a horse that way ought to be horse-whipped. When you get him unsaddled, help everyone else saddle horses."

Roger did as he was told and I was left with figuring out what would be suitable punishment for him. I had a number of options, but all of them were illegal. I finally decided to keep him around the stable and not let him guide or help guide any rides. By keeping him at the office, I would deny him the opportunity to make any money in tips. I'd hit him in the wallet, where I hoped it would hurt him most!

Doing Our Horse Training

Horses are creatures of habit. They learn by doing the same thing, the same way over and over. People learn the same way. It's important to keep repeating the lesson with a horse until he gets it down pat. Once he's learned one thing well a person can move onto another one.

I had a little mare that I was training on opening gates. She learned her lesson so well she would put herself in the proper position to open or close a gate, depending on what we were doing. Often, I had to hurry because she would start to move before I was ready. If she moved before I was ready, I could get my fingers or hand caught in the gate or fall off leaning too far to get the gate. I didn't like either one of the options.

At one horse rental stable where I worked the guests were expected to treat their rental horses as if they knew what they were doing. Of course, quite often, well, most often the guests didn't know what they were doing. Prior riding experience wasn't required to ride with us. Actually, all that was required was the money to go. Even though we gave fairly complete instructions, our instructions were often ignored. Sometimes I felt like I was talking to a brick wall when I gave the instructions. Even though I asked "Do you understand?" a short ride would prove that they hadn't listened.

I would always take the person's hand and move it in the direction I was showing them to turn to simulate neck reining.

With the women, when it was obvious that they hadn't paid attention, I would ask, "Do you want me to show you again?" I wouldn't give them a chance to answer, I'd say, "I'll show you again, I like holdin' hands with you!" And then repeat the instructions. Sometimes, but not all they time, it worked and they could turn and control the horse.

Of course the horses, being ridden so much by inexperienced riders, knew what they could get away with and what they couldn't. They also knew where we were going by the trail we headed out on. Quite often they were reluctant to head out on a particular trail knowing it was longer and they would have to carry the rider on their back longer.

If the horse didn't want to go, and start to turn back, I'd have to holler, "Turn him this way like I showed you. Kick him! He'll come if you show him who's boss!" Often this was a futile effort and I'd have to go back and lead the horse with the halter rope to get him to come.

Most commonly, the dude would say, "I don't want to hurt the horse."

"You can't really hurt this horse. He's about half smart," I'd say. And in my mind, I'd be thinking, *This is a case of the horse being smarter than the rider*. Occasionally, I'd think this a little out loud and get a dirty look from the guest. But it was true.

On this particular outfit they had a horse they called Bucky. Even though I never rode the horse, I didn't like him. He was a little longer in his back than I like and these longer-backed horses are supposed to be smoother riding. I didn't think he was, he didn't look like it. And he was a little more than half smart. I never really fully trusted the horse.

I always thought the riders for Bucky should have had a little experience behind them to ride him. The boss on the outfit, who matched the horses and riders, didn't feel this way.

On one particular day, the boss put a young lady on Bucky. She was a little overweight and I think the boss had a grudge against Bucky that day and this was his way of getting even with the horse. Or he could have taken a dislike to this young woman and wanted to show her a thing or two. I don't know. But I knew right from the start this was a mismatch.

The woman was obviously nervous about riding. I could tell it and so could Bucky. We started out and when we had gotten about a hundred yards away from the corral, Bucky decided he didn't want to go. He stopped and started to turn around. The woman screamed.

I had been watching and hollered, "Turn him around! He'll come!"

The woman made a feeble attempt to turn the horse but she wasn't successful. Bucky just stopped. He wasn't running, just walking, but the horse was giving the woman fits. Bucky had tried this before and when a person just got a little tough with him, he'd mind and follow along.

I rode back to be of help. When this had happened before, we'd managed to get Bucky lined out by convincing the rider to use what they considered to be a little force with him.

"I don't like this horse," cried the lady. "I don't want to go!" The woman was petrified. "I don't want to go," cried the woman again.

Out of the fear of losing all the other riders on the ride, I asked her, "Would you go if you had another horse?" I could see that Bucky had this woman buffaloed and would not have a good time.

"I don't like this horse!" The woman didn't answer my question; her fear of Bucky was so strong.

I don't like him either, I thought as I took the lead rope and started back to the barn to change horses.

The crew back at the barn had heard the scream and stopped whatever they were doing and came out to see what was going on. I got a dirty look from the boss as I led the woman into the yard.

"This lady don't like her horse," I said, as I handed the lead rope to the boss. "She'd like another horse."

"Go get Binky," said the boss, as he helped the woman off Bucky. One of the other hands brought out Binky, helped her on, adjusted her stirrups and we started out again.

The woman was still nervous about riding. "I want to be close to you," she said.

"Yes ma'am, I figured you'd need some watching," I said.

We continued the ride without incident and by the time we returned I think the lady was actually enjoying herself. When we got back and after the riders had left, the boss approached me.

"Stu," he said, "you shouldn't have brought that woman back. We'll have a hard time getting Bucky out in the future!"

"That's probably true," I said. "But Bucky had her number and she couldn't keep him following. I thought we'd lose all the riders on that ride when she said she didn't want to go."

"But you shouldn't have brought Bucky back. That will just impress on him that he doesn't have to go if he doesn't want to. That doesn't help with his training."

"That's true," I said. "But we really don't need the tourists doing our training for us!"

More Than What We Are

For some reason or other people always seem to want to add to or embellish their circumstances. I don't know why people do this; perhaps they are trying to improve their own self-image or impress someone else with their own worth.

I'd hired a young feller from Texas, his name was Jeff. He'd worked for me at a stable I managed in Grand Lake, Colorado. Now, I had my own rental horse stable and needed more help. Because he'd worked for me before, when he applied, I hired him immediately. I was already familiar with him.

I liked Jeff. He was personable, good with the dudes, and his horse skills were more than adequate. Although he was basically honest, he did tend to stretch the truth some. As he said, "It's a cowboy's right to never let the truth stand in the way of a good story!"

We were sitting around one afternoon waiting for a ride to return. We had all our chores done, we were caught up and didn't have anything pressing to do. We were just sitting there, throwing the "bull." Everybody had a story to tell and it seemed like each feller had to top the previous story.

I didn't join in on this "bull" session. I was content to just sit and listen.

Jeff was telling a story about riding a colt that didn't stop good. They used to chase coyotes and see if they could run them over a dropoff and watch them roll around when they hit the bottom. According to Jeff, this was a lot of fun because the coyotes would be watching over their shoulder when they were being chased and not watching where they were going,

He was on this colt, chasing a coyote and they came to a wash that was about ten or twelve feet deep and had a steep drop off. Jeff couldn't stop his colt and they went over the wash. Apparently all three of them, the coyote, the colt, and Jeff went over the wash and were rolling around in the bottom. They all emerged unhurt, although Jeff was sure the coyote and the colt had some bruises, just as he had.

I listened and the story sounded very familiar. I'd done about the same thing at a ranch I'd worked on in southern Idaho. I didn't say anything, I didn't think I could top Jeff's story. But although the story sounded very familiar, I thought it was possible two different guys could experience the same thing.

A few days later, Jeff came to me and said, "Do you remember that story I told a few days ago about chasing a coyote over a wash an' rollin' around in the bottom?"

"Yes," I said. Thinking that there was another "bull" session starting, I added, "I had something like that happen to me some years ago."

"Well," said Jeff, "you should be familiar with that story. It didn't happen to me. I read it in one of your books in the bunkhouse!"

R. LOREN SCHMIDT

Paying Attention

I was taking a break. The afternoon was hot and we had been fairly busy. All my hired help was out on rides and I was alone at my rental horse stables. The break was welcome; we had really been busy the previous few days. I had a soda pop and was seated in an easy chair in the shade in front of the office, where I could listen for the phone, watch the few horses in the corral, and be ready to help the tourists off the their horses when they returned. I was enjoying the rest and almost could have taken a nap.

The trail came right by the office where I was seated. Although it was our horse ride trail, it was often used by hikers and they would often stop on their hikes to rest and look at the horses. Occasionally, we would visit with these hikers and sometimes sell them a ride by saying, "You're doin' that the wrong way. You should ride one of our horses an' let them do the work! It's a lot more enjoyable, it's easier an' you can see more of the country when you're not havin' to watch where you're puttin' your feet."

On this particular day, a woman hiker, obviously tired, came and sat down in the empty chair beside me. After cordial greetings were exchanged, the woman started talking, about nothing in particular, just talking. She talked so much, I didn't have an opportunity to even try to sell her a ride. I didn't even have an opportunity to comment on what she was saying; she just went on and on and on. An occasional "Yep" was all I could fit in.

I was wishing that a ride would return or the phone would ring so I would have a legitimate excuse to leave. I was listening, but wasn't able to contribute anything to the conversation and wasn't getting much from her babbling. Finally some other hikers came by and stopped for a few minutes.

"It looks like you folks have the best seats in the country," said one of the new arrivals.

"Yep," I said.

The woman said, "This nice man was just sitting here and I came up and have been talking his head off and tiring him out ever since I got here."

"Don't worry about it, lady," I said. "I ain't been listening."

Apologetic

I needed more horses for our rental horse operation. We had around a hundred head, but we had gotten busy, and I was working the horses I had harder than I wanted to. I'd been to all the horse sales in the area during the spring and early summer, but hadn't been able to buy many. Those horses I bought were older horses and I figured I'd just use them one year then sell them. If I could get the purchase price out of them in the fall, what money they made for the business could be applied to feed, wages and overhead. Hopefully there would be some left over for me.

There were a lot of horses for sale, but the prices were higher than I wanted to pay and didn't figure into the formula I had worked out to make money on a horse purchase. I hadn't allowed for inflation in my formula and to adjust the formula, I would need to increase the prices of the hourly rides, two-hour rides, half-day rides, and our food rides. I really didn't want to do that after our summer season had started as our brochures were already printed and I would need to get permission from the resort where we were operating to raise prices. We were concessionaires at the resort and our prices had been mutually agreed on when we negotiated our operating contract. I was stuck between a rock and a hard spot.

I contacted a horse trader close to Durango, Colorado. I had bought horses from him in the past and for the most part, the horses had worked out well and the prices were reasonable. However, Hal had leased out most of his horses and didn't have any for sale. He did have a few, around twenty head that he could lease to me. He couldn't sell them as he needed them for the hunting season in the fall.

I really like to see the horses ridden before I buy them so I have some idea of what I'm buying. I had never leased horses before but I had bought horses from Hal in the past, they worked well and I had come to trust Hal. I leased the horses over the phone. Hal explained the terms of his lease agreement to me and we made arrangements to have the horses delivered. I would have to return the horses after Labor Day.

The horses arrived; I paid Hal the lease fee and was pleased with what we had got after we tried them out. I really wished I could have bought them. We used the horses all summer and they really lightened the workload on my own horses. All the horses earned their keep that summer.

Labor Day came, our business slowed down because school started and the families had to have their kids in school. We still did some hourly rides, but mostly to retired people and families that home-schooled their children. I started to haul horses to the winter ranch to save on feed at the stables. I hauled the horses that had worked the hardest to the winter ranch first. The time came to take the leased horses back to Durango.

My oldest son, Will, had purchased a semi-tractor and trailer and he agreed to take the leased horses back. We got a brand inspection, loaded the horses early one morning and sent Will on his way. It was a long day's drive to Durango and if everything went well, Will should be back the following night.

When Will got back the next day, I asked him, "How did your trip go? The horses travel all right?"

"Not exactly," replied Will.

"What happened?"

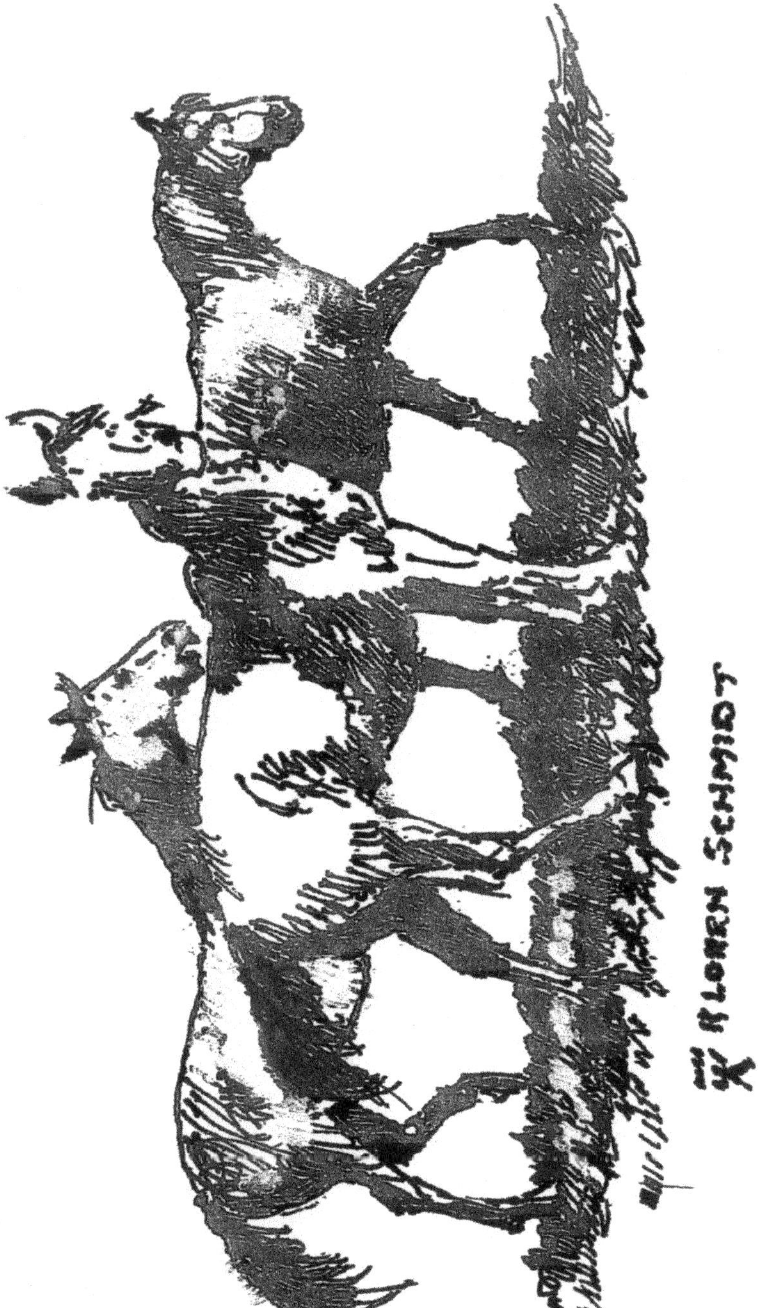

"One of the horses got down. I heard some struggling in the trailer, stopped and went back to check. The horse we called 'Pig' got down. I had to cut the lead rope so she could get up. I was afraid she'd die if she stayed down. That was all I could do because she'd pulled the lead rope so tight, I couldn't get it undone."

"That's all right son," I answered. The thoughts of what I had to pay to Hal to replace a horse that had died while in my care raced through my mind.

"I didn't want to do it, but that's all I could do," said Will. "I'm sorry I cut your lead rope."

Will seemed more concerned with destroying my halter than with saving the horse and kept apologizing for his action. The halter and lead rope were braided together and to cut the lead rope rendered the halter useless.

"Will," I said, "don't worry about cutting the lead rope. It had to be done. You need to take into consideration the difference between the cost of replacing the horse and replacing the halter. You saved us a lot of money, so don't worry about it."

But Will did worry about it and he kept apologizing for cutting the halter. He apologized so much that I got tired hearing it. Finally, after apologizing again, I said, "Forget about cutting the lead rope. I'm getting tired of hearing it. But, if it will make you feel better I'll deduct the cost of the halter from your wages!"

Will stopped apologizing for cutting the lead rope.

Cleanliness

Work around horses is dirty. There's no getting around it. Hay is dirty and dusty. Manure is dirty. Horses roll in the dirt and brushing them off is dirty. It's hard to stay clean when working around horses.

I used to enjoy watching the girls we hired coming to work. The first few days on the job the girls were sorta dressed up; as dressed up as a person can get in blue jeans, and every strand of their hair was properly in place. Their makeup was applied and perfect. This was particularly true of the girls we hired that didn't have much experience with horses. After a few days their hair was combed but not so perfect and the makeup was not applied as diligently. The girls soon came to realize that this was dirty work.

One girl, and I have long since forgotten her name, did apply her own personal touch, although her makeup wasn't worn. She always showed up with a neckerchief or wild rag that was as color-coordinated as our tan uniform shirts would allow. She maintained her style of dress all summer long.

At another stable, a young lady asked me the question, "How do you keep your fingernails clean?"

"I don't know," I replied. "I don't much worry about mine."

"But how do you keep the dirt out from underneath them?"

"Well," I answered, "when you shower at night, wash your

hair and use your fingers to get the dirt out. Or you could wear gloves."

"I know that about showering. And I can't do anything with gloves on," she replied. "But how do you keep the dirt out from underneath them during the day?"

"That's pretty hard to do, pert near impossible. You can clean them often with a toothpick or fingernail cleaner."

"Why that's almost a constant manicure," she exclaimed.

"That's what it takes," I said. "Of course you could simply admit that it's impossible and learn to live with the situation."

"That's kinda like giving in, isn't it?"

"I guess it would be," I admitted. "But you could cover up the problem."

"How?"

"First, you admit there's a problem. Second, you admit you don't have a solution. Third, you paint your fingernails. No, you don't get rid of the dirt, but you hide it from everyone. With your fingernails painted, only you will know there's dirt under them. It will be up to you to keep them clean. Of course, I'll know, but I ain't going to tell anybody."

"I think that's what I'll do! Thanks Stu!"

My advice was taken and she showed up for work the next day with her fingernails painted. I still find it hard to believe that an old cowboy like myself is qualified to give beauty tips to college girls!

Misunderstanding?

I spent a few years working for the same outfit. In the summer we did the guided one- and two-hour horseback rides for the tourists. Occasionally, we'd have to do a four-hour ride for the more adventuresome tourists.

In the winter, we'd do sleigh rides. The sleigh rides were done in the late afternoon or early evening and it was a lot colder than the hourly rides we did during the summer.

One winter, it seemed particularly slower than other years. I wondered if it would be a profitable winter. We had done sleigh rides, but I was probably the only hand that tried to compare the business to other years.

Before the end of the sleigh ride season the boss called us together and announced, "We'll have one big sleigh ride before we're done. I've made a deal with the resort to transport their guests to the convention center on Thursday night, between eight and nine o'clock. We'll get five hundred dollars whether we take one person or a hundred, and it's only about a hundred-yard sleigh ride. This will make our year!"

Thursday came and we harnessed three teams of horses, hitched them to three sleighs and went to the meeting place to pick up the tourists. There were only about twenty people waiting for sleigh rides. We took them to the convention center, got them unloaded then went back to the meeting place to see if there were any stragglers. There weren't. We waited an appropriate amount of time then headed back to the barn. The whole affair only lasted about an hour.

On the way back, the boss, who was in the lead sleigh, yelled back at me, "That's the easiest six hundred dollars I ever made!"

I didn't say anything, but I did recall being told that we were doing the deal for five hundred dollars.

While we were un-harnessing the horses, the boss said, "That was a pretty easy seven hundred dollars we made tonight. I wish every night was that good!"

I still didn't say anything, but remembered the five hundred dollar deal growing to six hundred dollars and now it was at seven.

A few days later the sleigh rides were over. We took on some extra work. Then one day the boss showed up and looked somewhat down.

I asked, "What's the matter?"

"Remember that sleigh ride we did a few days ago?"

"Yep," I replied.

"Well, I sent the resort a bill for seven hundred dollars and they shorted me. They only made the check for five hundred dollars. It's just like a large business, taking advantage of a small business just to line their own pockets!"

The boss was quite adamant about the situation. I didn't say anything, but I distinctly remembered the five hundred dollar deal. The whole thing looked like to me that the little guy was trying to take advantage of the larger guy, the exact opposite of what the boss was accusing the resort of doing to him.

A short time later, the boss and I had a falling out and I quit. Although the sleigh ride incident was in the back of my mind, our falling out was over another matter.

I find it hard to maintain a high standard when management of the company I'm working for does not honor its own deals.

Lean Left!

On one dude outfit, we had a horse that was kinda hard to handle. He was hard to get on and when a person got on him, he couldn't be counted on to do what he'd been asked to do. A pretty good-looking horse, the boss wanted to teach him how to be a good horse. Someone hadn't started the horse very well and he pretty much did what he wanted.

The boss, Dave, had us catch the horse one day, and after some groundwork, had one of the girls get on him while he held the horse. Dave's idea was to have the horse circle close around him with the girl riding the horse. As the horse behaved and found out what Dave wanted, Dave would play out more lead rope, giving the horse more freedom.

I didn't think much of the idea, but I always thought Dave knew what he was doing with the horses. Things went well until the girl got in the saddle.

When the horse felt the full weight of the girl on his back, he didn't much appreciate it and tried to buck. Dave had control of his head and the horse couldn't buck. But he could move and he started circling around Dave, circling to the left. The horse couldn't get his head down and do a good job of bucking, Dave had a good hold on him. But he could move and kick out his hind feet.

Being able to kick out his hind feet loosened the girl in the saddle. She started to lean to the right and she got looser every jump. I thought I might get behind her on the outside and push her back in the saddle, but decided against it. Running behind the horse would only make the horse go faster and Dave had his hands full trying to control the horse.

Besides that, I was on the outside of the circle and would have farther to run. And I stood the chance of getting kicked by the horse. All I could do was stay out of the way and holler, "Lean left! Lean left!"

My advice to the girl went unheeded. Either she didn't hear me or she was too far out of the saddle to regain her balance, so she fell off.

She wasn't hurt, just some minor bruises. I helped her out of the corral and sent her to the bunkhouse to get cleaned up.

When the girl fell off, the horse stopped his contrary actions. Dave continued to move the horse in a circle around him. Soon, he stopped.

We turned the horse loose and went to the cook shack for our noon meal. On the way, Dave said, "I thought I could hold him!"

Well, he couldn't and it left me wondering, *Why didn't he snub the unruly horse to him like we used to?* To this day, I still don't know.

Evolution

Things have changed over the years. A lot of the old methods have given way to new methods in breaking and training horses and equipment. Of course a horse will always be a horse and a saddle always a saddle. Some things will never change.

The changes in our vocabulary have presented me with some peculiar problems. The word "ain't" has become commonplace much to what would be the dismay of my mother. I would love to be able to tell her, "See, I was right all these years!" But that won't happen.

I've had to be careful in using language around our horse rental customers. Some things are permissible and some are not. I've always taken the attitude that when a prospect for a horse ride approaches, we don't have anything yet, so we don't have anything to lose. So I can say just about anything. I've learned that a person can say just about anything to the general public; it's not what you say that counts, its how you say it. I've had a lot of fun joking with our prospective customers and the humor tends to put a lot of people that are somewhat apprehensive about riding at ease. They tend to relax in a humorous atmosphere.

However, because some of our words are taking on a different meaning, I've had to change my speech, although the meanings are the same to me.

For example, when I was in the army some years ago, shower

shoes were referred to as "thongs." They're not called that any more. I got into trouble referring to shower shoes as thongs when I would tell our riders what kind of footwear was not acceptable. I would say, "You can't ride barefooted, or with high-heeled spiked shoes, or sandals, or thongs."

Quite often, the customer would ask, "Why not?"

My reply was simple, "It's not safe."

Of course, when I said "thongs," I was referring to shower shoes. The customers thought I was referring to something else.

Apparently, the word "thong" has evolved to mean skimpy underwear. I wondered why I would get some funny looks from the customers as I said that. I was even asked once by a lady customer determined to ride if we had a place they could change.

It wasn't until I was informed by one of the other wranglers what "thongs" meant that I realized my errors.

Today, I still have thongs, they are shower shoes; they are not skimpy underwear. I call them flip-flops now.

Partners

I figured I had about the biggest work horse in Grand County, Colorado. Of course I hadn't seen all the work horses in Grand County, but Dick was clearly bigger than any of the work horses I had seen. There were days when I wished he wasn't so big; it was tough to throw harness on him, especially on cold winter days.

I had a rental horse stable and Dick and Jane were a team we used for sleigh rides in the winter and wagon rides in the summer. They were a good, honest team and I liked them a lot. I had some other teams and we used each team on a rotation basis. But Dick and Jane were the best.

I'd bought them from a friend of mine some years previously over in western Colorado. I'd known Duke for a few years and more than one person had told me, "You can go to the bank with anything Duke says."

One year, I needed more leader ponies. We kept a number of ponies available so that parents could lead the kids around that were too young to ride their own horses on our trail rides. We couldn't allow any double riding, so the leader ponies were necessary so that the younger children could have a horse experience. It worked out well when I could find the right kind of ponies.

But I had a hard time finding the right ponies. I needed to pick ponies based on disposition rather than breed. I wanted ponies that could be led, with a small child on their back, by a parent that didn't know anything about horses. I needed ponies that wouldn't bite the leader, or kick side-walkers while they were on their pony walk, or try to run off or back to the barn when they got a couple of hundred yards away from the corrals.

I generally had to try out three or four ponies before I would find one that would work out for our use. The Shetland pony was the right size, but all too often, their disposition wasn't compatible with our needs. A lot of this was probably due to the humans handling them. Because of their small size, many of the ponies weren't handled correctly. The trainers weren't firm enough with them as they were being trained, consequently, they got away with a lot and developed some bad habits. I needed them to be dependable and honest from the first day. We didn't have time to teach them new ways or retrain them to break them of their bad habits.

At a horse sale one day, a miniature horse came through. The auctioneer proclaimed the miniature to be "broke to ride an' drive an' plumb gentle to boot!"

Taking a chance, I bid on the horse. There wasn't much bidding action and I ended up buying the small horse. I hadn't been able to purchase any other horses at the sale and the yard man laughed as he saw me drive up pulling a twenty-four-foot gooseneck horse trailer behind the truck.

"This the only horse you bought today, Stu?"

"Yep," I answered.

"Well," said the yard man, "he ought to have enough room in that trailer!" He was laughing as he handed me the lead rope.

"Yep," I said as I took the lead rope and tied the horse to the front of the trailer. "I like for my horses to have plenty of room."

As I got in the truck and started to drive away, I noticed the yard man in my rearview mirrors, still laughing. I had to laugh a little myself; I did have plenty of trailer for one miniature horse!

I was a little concerned as to what I was going to do with the miniature horse when I got home. I had plenty of corral space, but I didn't have separate corrals where I could isolate new horses for a few days until they became acquainted with the rest of the herd. I decided I'd tie the miniature outside and carry hay to him. I'd wire a bucket to the fence for water then in a few days, turn him in with the rest of the horses and hope for the best.

After three days of keeping the miniature tied outside the corral at night and using him as a leader pony during the day, I decided to turn him into the big corral.

I shouldn't have worried. As soon as I turned him loose in the big corral, Dick, the big work horse, came over, nuzzled him and they both went to the feed bunk to eat. Apparently, they had become acquainted through the fence and had become good friends. In fact, it appeared that Dick had become the miniature's guardian.

The two horses—the biggest and the smallest—had become a topic of conversation, even among the tourists. Often, when we were leaving the corrals in the evening, we would see tourists petting the miniature and Dick through the fence. When one horse would go to the fence to be petted by the tourists, the other would follow.

I often thought I would like to harness Dick and harness the miniature, hook them to the wagon and go for a ride. I never did that because I didn't have a horse collar or harness small enough to fit the miniature. I would have liked to do it, just for the fun of it. I would have taken a picture of it and called it "Partners."

Knowin' It All

As a young teenager, I thought I knew quite a bit about horses and cattle. I never got real "cocky" about it, although I felt free to express my opinions about horses and cattle and often my opinions amused the old timers. I suppose they enjoyed more than a few good laughs at my expense.

Having had a good deal of experience at my young age, I applied for a job at a dude and cattle ranch in Montana and got it. I didn't know that a dude wrangler position required good people skills more so than good horse and cattle skills. I really didn't know how much I had to learn.

When I arrived at the ranch, I was greeted by the owner and his wife. I had my own saddle and that fact, I thought, enhanced my image in the eyes of my new employer. I was shown the bunkhouse. I was the only hired hand, so the place was all mine. At supper that night, the daily routine was laid out before me. I was to get up early, go to each one of the guest's cabins and light the wood-burning stove so the dudes would have some heat to get dressed with. Then I was to saddle the jingle horse and gather the dude horses.

I remember the name of the jingle horse, Banner, and the name of the owner, Jim, but I can't remember the name of his wife. Jim's wife was very adamant about tightening the cinches on the dude horses.

"The dudes tend to pull themselves up on the saddle," she said. "If the cinches aren't tight enough, they'll pull the saddle over when they get on. If they do make it on, the saddle is liable to roll with them while they're riding. In either case, somebody hits the ground."

The next morning, my first day on the job, Jim came with me to light the stoves. Then we saddled a couple of horses and gathered the dude horses. Jim pointed out where some horses would hide out and try to get out of working for the day. When the horses were gathered, we went to breakfast.

Jim's wife again stressed the importance of tightening the cinches on the dude horses.

A couple of days later, the dudes started arriving and we saddled most of the dude horses. The first horse I saddled was a fat mare without much withers on her. Remembering Jim's wife's warnings, I tightened the cinch as tight as I could get it, and went to saddle another horse. I guess I had pulled the cinch too tight,

because when I returned to saddle another horse, the fat mare was laying down, kicking her feet in the air.

Jim had seen what was happening and rushed to get the horse up and get her to her feet.

"That's plenty tight," he said. "It's a little too tight."

He loosened the cinch, much to the relief of the mare.

Sometimes we try too hard to show how much we know when we don't know much. It just goes to prove how little we actually do know.

Bucket

At a rental horse stable in Colorado, I got hired on, mostly through the efforts of some friends of mine. I'd done some work on a dude ranch in Montana quite a few years earlier, and although I'd have preferred to work on a regular cow outfit, I couldn't find work close to home. So, I turned my own saddle horse loose in a pasture that I figured had enough feed to last him all summer, locked the house, got my saddle and bedroll, left Utah and went to Grand Lake, Colorado.

I didn't really know what to expect on this new job. My friend who was instrumental in getting me the job assured me I could handle the position. Her son, Steve, was the manager of the stable.

I arrived in Grand Lake in the late afternoon, put my bedroll in the bunkhouse and listened as Steve explained the operation of the outfit. It appeared to be pretty simple. My job was to run a little satellite stable up on the hill in conjunction with the Grand Lake Lodge Company.

Steve explained, "We don't really sell a lot of horse rides at the lodge. We actually maintain a small stable there to be able to use the trail across their property to gain access into the National Park. I generally use it to 'hide out' some lame horses. We only keep about ten head up there."

Steve told me how I could ride a horse to the stable every day, taking a short cut, after helping saddle the horses and come back about four in the afternoon to help unsaddle and leave my truck at the main stable. The next morning I helped saddle the horses at the main stable then Steve pointed out a horse I could saddle and use. I saddled him and rode up to the satellite stable.

I looked over the string of ten horses I had to operate with. Steve had told me which horses took what kind of riders and I saddled eight of the horses. Two horses were lame and I couldn't use them.

I didn't have an opportunity to ride the trails I was supposed to use; Steve simply told me where they were. The trails were in the National Park and were well marked.

I sold a few rides that day and learned the trails while I was taking rides out. It was really simple. I was riding a different horse every day up to my little stable and about three days later, Steve gave me "Bucket," a horse to use every day.

"Bucket," said Steve "is a mustang out of Wyoming. He's a real fast walker and going up that hill every day will help slow him down. He's too much horse to rent to the dudes. He does tend to shy quite a bit."

I saddled Bucket and rode him up to the little stable. He'd never been up there before and shied at everything. But he did walk fast. I hate to slow down a fast-walking horse, but it was part of the job. I figured he'd stop shying at everything when he'd been up the hill a few times and had gotten used to it.

I sold a lot of rides at that little stable, a lot more than the other people who had been sent up to do it. I thought that the hired help that had been sent up to watch it just used the time there to catch up on their sleep. I sold enough rides that Steve finally took the lame horses back to the main stable and gave me some horses that I could use.

I'd unsaddle at about three-thirty in the afternoon and ride down to the main stable to help unsaddle there. After the Fourth of July, we rented a night pasture where we could turn out some horses overnight and cut down on our feed bill at the stable. The night pasture was about a mile and a half east of the stable, on the other side of the Town of Grand Lake, and the horses had to be "jingled" up there each night and gathered each morning.

Due to a late ride I'd scheduled at my stable, I missed jingling the horses to the night pasture the first night we used it, but was up earlier the next morning to gather the horses with two other hands.

We gathered the horses into a little corral. When we were satisfied we had all the horses, I took the lead to take the horses back to the stable. Going through the trees along the road was pretty simple. We started out at a good trot, but when we got out of the trees, I could feel Bucket tense up. I looked around thinking there might be a bear or something along the side of the road to spook him, but couldn't see anything.

Bucket started to slow down and I had to spur him to keep him going. I couldn't see what was bothering him, but I kept him going. We reached the stable without further incident, although Bucket shied a few more times on the way. Bucket seemed to relax when we reached the corrals.

I made it down from my little stable that night early enough to help jingle the horses to the night pasture. Once again, I led the horses and out in the middle of the road, Bucket tensed up again. I couldn't see what was making him nervous, but we made it to the night pasture.

Going back to the stable, Bucket seemed relaxed all the way. I thought if there was something alongside the road, he'd get nervous at about the same spot where he tensed up that morning and afternoon. But nothing happened.

The next morning, I gathered horses again. Bucket was good going up to the night pasture, but coming back, he got tense at the same area where he'd tensed up the morning before. It took me a while, but I finally figured it out.

Coming back from the night pasture in the morning, the sun was at our backs, low in the sky. Bucket and I cast a long shadow in the morning and Bucket was afraid of his own shadow! The reverse was true in the afternoon. I tested my theory by raising an arm and waving it around. The shadow moved and Bucket really shied—I almost lost him.

I decided I'd help Bucket get over his fear by weaving back and forth on the way to and from the night pasture. That way, he'd see his shadow on both sides of him and might figure out that it couldn't hurt him. Of course if it didn't work, things might get worse!

It took some doing, but we finally got Bucket accustomed to seeing his own shadow early in the morning and late in the afternoon.

First Day on the Job

I was the new hand on the outfit, and probably the most experienced, even though I hadn't ridden any of the trails. I'd been riding long before most of the help was even born.

It was my first day and I was aware everyone was watching me, waiting for me to make some sort of mistake. I'm afraid they were disappointed. I'd worked for outfits that used a saddling chute before and although some outfits had varying procedures, saddling a horse was fairly basic.

I was given a horse that was new to the outfit to ride and I didn't think much of him. He was fairly green and I didn't know what to expect. Before any of the day's riders arrived, I got on the horse and rode him around just to see what I had. He was a snaffle bit horse and although he didn't know much, I figured I could do what I needed to do on him. Some of the hired help was surprised when I cheeked the horse when I got on him, some didn't know what I was doing. I've always cheeked strange horses when I first got on them and just because this was a dude outfit, I didn't see any reason to change.

The outfit was managed by a retired army officer. He ran a fairly strict outfit with some definite rules, primarily of which was that all the rides should leave on time and get back on time. Secondly, no one was to lose his or her horse out on the trail.

For about two hundred yards, the departure trail and the

return trail were the same. If a ride left late and met a returning ride, a lot of the departing horses would simply turn around and follow the incoming ride back to the barn, figuring, no doubt, that they'd had a pretty short work day. Prior riding experience wasn't required to ride with us and the dudes would just let their horses return, even though they'd been given instructions on how to control their horses.

The second rule didn't bother me much. I've never lost my horse on these dude rides. For one thing, it generally meant a long walk back to the barn and I wasn't in favor of that. Another thing that could be counted on: to come walking in on foot leading a dude horseback ride would be mighty embarrassing and would lead to a lot of harassment in the future. I'd seen it happen on other outfits and had been a part of the harassment team. I'd had a lot of fun at someone else's expense.

The main reason the boss didn't want anyone to lose their horse out on the trail was that most horses, when they figured out they were free would head toward the barn, sometimes at a walk, grazing as they went, but quite often at a dead run. If the loose horse met another ride, and went running by them, a lot of the dude horses would turn and follow at a dead run, often leaving their riders on the ground. On this outfit, losing your horse was grounds for immediate dismissal. And the boss made this very clear.

I was selected to accompany Arturo on the first ride of the day, more to learn the trail than to be of any real help. This was a courtesy extended to me by the boss, being the new hand. It wasn't really needed, the trail was four or five wide in most places, well defined with plenty of horse manure and horse tracks.

On this ride, Arturo was having a rough time with one woman. She was quite demanding and was constantly dropping something—her camera, glasses, scarf and whatever. She constantly talked and most of the time her talk didn't have anything to do with the country or the ride. She was constantly needing her stirrups or saddle adjusted.

Every time she dropped something, Arturo had to stop the ride, get off his horse and pick it up. He was becoming quite perturbed and disgusted with the woman and he wasn't doing a very good job of hiding it from her. At one point, when the woman dropped her camera, Arturo didn't give it back to her. She'd dropped it three or four times and Arturo was getting tired of getting off, picking it up and giving it back to her, then getting back on his horse.

"I'll just hold onto this until we get back," he said. "Just for safe keeping."

"You'll give it back when we get done," said the woman. "Won't you?"

"Certainly," replied Arturo, hanging the camera by its strap over the saddle horn.

Arturo got back on his horse and the ride proceeded.

Every time the woman needed something, Arturo would get off his horse and do whatever was necessary. Each time the ride stopped, I would leave the tail end and ride up to see what was the matter and offer my help. I could see Arturo was becoming very frustrated.

"Want me to lead the ride?" I was trying to be helpful.

"No," replied Arturo. "We're about halfway done. I'll handle it from here."

"Suit yourself," I said and returned to the tail end of the ride where I'd been visiting with some of the riders.

As I rode past the riders, some of them asked, "What's happening up there?"

I was honest with the guests. "Arturo's having a rough time with that woman up there. But everything is all right."

"I know he's having a tough time with her," said one man. "That's my wife!"

I decided to change the topic of conversation after that comment.

Arturo had to stop a couple of more times. I didn't ride up to see if I could help, I hadn't been of any help previously.

On one of these occasions, I remained at the rear of the ride, watching what was going on up ahead. All of the sudden, I saw Arturo's horse shy and trot away a few yards. Arturo was in hot pursuit, which caused the horse to trot farther away. The horse wasn't running, just trotting, staying far enough away from Arturo that he couldn't catch him.

I made a big circle around the riders and approached Arturo.

"What happened?"

"My horse got away from me," answered Arturo.

I found out later that Arturo was in the habit of dropping his reins while he did whatever he had to on foot, figuring his horse would stand ground-tied until he needed him.

"I'll see if I can catch your horse," I said as I made a big circle around the loose horse.

As I left, I heard Arturo muttering, supposedly under his breath, but loud enough to be heard by the woman, "I'll probably lose my job over this. If you're going to drop anything, lady, now's the time to do it, I'm already on foot."

I thought Arturo's comments were out of line and wondered if he was just talking in order to increase his chances of a tip. I didn't worry about it, I had to catch his horse.

The horse was walking, grazing as he went. The reins were dragging on the ground. I got ahead of the horse and when he saw me he wheeled and made a right angle turn. The reins went flying around and when the horse's feet came down, his feet were in the reins. He'd caught himself. Arturo used a company bridle and the reins on all the company bridles were knotted. Dudes have a habit of dropping their reins, and knotted reins helped prevent

any disasters from happening. The boss and I were the only ones on this outfit that rode with split reins.

I got off my horse, took the horse's feet out from the reins, got back on my horse and led Arturo's horse back to the ride. Arturo was on foot, of course, leading the ride back. I hadn't been gone more than ten minutes and Arturo hadn't made much progress. I gave him the horse and he took the reins without a comment, got on and the ride proceeded.

I rode to the tail end of the ride thinking, *Not even a thanks! I saved him a long walk, I saved his job and not even a thanks!*

He did provide some humorous moments however. We were putting the dudes on their horses one morning and I heard Arturo ask a woman, "Are you ready to be mounted?"

The woman nodded her head and Arturo got her on her horse. I could hardly keep a straight face. The term "mounted" has a completely different meaning in the horse world.

Arturo proved to be kinda difficult to get along with. Knowing what I know now, I would have let him walk back on foot that day. But it was my first day on the job.

Herdin' Chickens

When I had the cow ranch out in eastern Utah, we tried to grow all the food we needed on the ranch. We killed a beef every year, although it wasn't a prime or even choice beef. It was generally an older open cow. Consequently we ate a lot of hamburger. We had a milk cow and made a lot of our own butter from the Jersey cow. We had a garden one year, but discontinued it when I found my son Sam eating peas, right out of the pod in the garden.

We also raised some chickens. They were sent to us via a mail-order house and they arrived, all of them alive! I was surprised. Not a one had died during shipment. There were a hundred! I did feel sorry for the postmaster at the post office. She had to listen to them all day until I got off work in town and could pick them up.

I brought the chicks home and went back to town to get a heat lamp to keep them at a comfortable temperature. The instructions that were enclosed with the chicks said we needed a heat lamp and we could tell if the chicks were too hot or cold by how they spaced themselves under the heat lamp.

I also bought some chicken feed at the feed store where I got the heat lamp. We kept the chickens in the house for a time, but when the house started to smell, I decided to move them outside. This presented a problem because I hadn't finished building a proper chicken coop. I had plenty to do, taking care of my own cows, doing my job in town and doing my regular chores. My wife at the time—I've had four four of them—wasn't much good at helping with the chores, trying to take care of her kids, our kid, and doing the cooking. So all the farm work was left to me.

I did spend a lot of time watching the chicks at night before I went to bed and watched how they established their pecking order.

I wasn't sure just how to provide housing for the chickens that would keep them warm. But I did have a camper shell for the pickup. I figured I could run an extension cord from the house to the camper shell to provide heat for the chicks and that would get them out of the house. I'd leave the tailgate up so the chicks could have free access to their new house. This idea worked pretty well for a time, but before long, they outgrew the camper shell. I had to get the chicken coop completed!

At my wife's continued instance, one Saturday afternoon I finally completed the coop, chicken wire and all. Now we had to catch them and put them in their new home. I figured the next day, Sunday, would be a good time to do that. I figured we could capture most of the chicks under the camper shell and get the kids to get them and put them in their new home.

But my wife wouldn't go for that. "Do you expect my children to crawl around in all that chicken manure to catch chickens?"

My wife didn't exactly use that language, but her meaning was perfectly clear.

"That's the way I had it figured," I said.

"Well, my kids aren't going to do that!"

So I asked, "How do you propose to get the chicks from the camper shell to the coop?"

"We can herd them," answered my wife. It seemed like she had an answer for everything.

"I've never heard of herdin' chickens," I said.

"They herd turkeys, don't they?"

"I've heard they do, but I've never done it," I said.

"Well, if people can herd turkeys, we can herd chickens. We only have to go around the house and into the chicken coop."

"I don't think it'll work," I said.

"It will work," said my wife. "We'll make it work. Besides that, you tell me you're a cowboy, and a darn good one. If you're as good a cowboy as you say you are, you ought to be able to do it. Cowboys can herd anything!" With some doubt, I consented. I admit I may have layed it on a little thick about how good a cowboy I was, and I was beginning to regret it.

I asked, trying to be humorous, "Will I need my horse?"

RLOREN SCHMIDT

"Don't be silly," she retorted. "We only have to take them thirty feet or so. The kids can help."

I had an idea we were biting off more than we could chew, but, armed with the kids on either side of me and the wife on one end, we started to gather the chickens.

Normally, livestock will move directly away from you when you approach them. Not so with chickens. They'll move any direction. It's hard to keep them in a herd. And if you try to press them, they'll fly right over your head.

When we had the chicks scattered all over the front yard, the wife hollered, "Hold it! Hold it! We're going about this the wrong way. I'll get some feed and we'll bait them into the coop."

The kids and I waited until the wife brought some feed and spilled a path to the coop. She must have put out a week's worth of food laying a path to the coop.

We tried the scheme again, without success. The chicks wouldn't follow the feed trail. I'd had chickens running to the right of me and chickens running to the left of me and even a few flying over my head. I found myself ducking when they flew over me. Trying to catch a few, I took off my hat and waved it fruitlessly at the fleeing chicks. After a few tries full of effort, the kids were tired and I was beginning to see failure written all over this project.

The kids were beat, the wife was beat and even I had to admit defeat. We gave up. I thought it would be easier to hunt for eggs the chickens laid out in the open than to continue to try and herd chickens into the coop.

Nothing was said about our chicken herding experience for a few days. Then, when I got home from work one day, my wife proudly announced that she had captured the chickens.

"And just how did you do that?"

"I just put the feed and water in the coop and eventually they found it," said my wife. "It was a lot easier than you trying to herd them into the coop."

"Herdin' the chickens wasn't my idea in the first place," I said. "As I recall, you hatched up that scheme all by yourself! I'm surprised you talked me into it!"

"But you were willing."

Conserving Water

The Anthro Mountains in eastern Utah is a hot, dry, open range. There isn't much water, but there's a lot of grass. The Ute Indian tribe runs some of their cattle on the mountain along with some other ranchers.

I hired on one summer to watch their cattle. There were two of us punchers, Almy and me. Occasionally the cow boss would show up to give us a hand, but he preferred working with the Indians up in the Uinta Mountains where it was cooler. Almy and I had our hands full. Some days we couldn't get our work done.

The cow boss hired another hand to help us out. He was new to the country and hadn't ridden it before.

Somebody had devised an ingenious method of conserving water and providing water for the cattle all up and down the mountain. There was a spring on top of the mountain and it flowed freely year-round. Someone had devised a method of catching the overflow from the watering trough on top of the mountain and piping it down to another trough down the mountain apiece. A series of water troughs were linked together in just such a manner and water was available for the cattle. In some places the pipe was above the ground and in other places it was only six inches or so below the ground.

The pipe, being plastic PVC pipe, had to be constantly checked in case the cattle had broken it or otherwise knocked it

loose. Before we put cattle on the mountain, we rode the pipeline looking for breaks. As the summer progressed, we moved cattle higher up on the mountain periodically, leaving them on water at the end of the day. There were some areas fenced off, so we didn't have to re-gather the cattle we had already moved. Because of the vastness of each pasture, we had to re-ride each pasture periodically. By the middle of summer, we had cattle scattered all over the mountain, but the idea was to have them all on top. So we had a lot of riding to do and it was all hot and dusty.

Pushing cattle up the mountain was really rough and both horses and men got tired quickly. And the summer heat didn't add any comfort.

Our new hand fit in well. He'd done a lot of work with cattle and had rode quite a bit. But he didn't know the country.

On one particularly hot day, we pushed cattle to one water trough and let them water good, then started them toward the next pasture. Before we left the water trough, the new hand rode up to it, let his horse drink, then got off and took a drink from where the pipe emptied into the trough.

Almy and I looked at each other and grinned.

"Interest you boys in a drink? It's cold," said the new hand, stepping back from the trough and wiping his chin with his shirt-sleeve.

"I'm good," I said.

"So am I," said Almy.

"You boys must be used to this country and the hot, dry conditions."

"We know the country an' the piping system for the water. It comes from the other water troughs higher up an' it prob'ly contains a lot of cow slobber and other stuff cows leave in water troughs."

The new hand looked amazed. "Really?"

"Yep," said Almy. "I hope you don't get sick. Stu an' I will get a drink at the top."

The new hand looked a little sick at Almy's comment, but got back on his horse.

A Fashion Statement

Clothes to most cowboys just need to be tough and serviceable. To most cowboys, working out on big cow outfits, it doesn't make much difference what a feller looks like. His clothes are most likely to be sweat-stained, wrinkled and dirty at the end of the day anyway. And if he has to, or chooses to, he might wear the same clothes for a few days in a row. Who's going to notice? Probably the same guys he worked with yesterday and more than likely, they'll be wearing the same clothes they wore the day before yesterday. Out on the ranch, it doesn't make much difference.

But when a cowboy goes to town, that's likely to make a difference. A cowboy will have his best clothes on, and do the best he can to keep them clean.

It makes little difference to those cowboys who have spent a lot of time out on the ranch, if they do get duded up when they go to town. As long as they're clean they don't care if they look like a dude. A feller might want to be careful to call one of them a "dude," that might lead to some problems.

In the dude business, it's a little different. All the hands—dude wranglers—are expected to look clean and sharp all the time, regardless of the weather or what conditions they're working in.

I remember one outfit I worked on in Colorado. It was a rainy year and there was a lot of mud in the corrals. It was hard to go

in the corrals and catch a horse without getting muddy, consequently all the hands looked dirty all the time.

The owner of this outfit lived on the other side of the Rocky Mountains, close to Denver. One morning, after a big rainstorm the previous afternoon, he showed up unexpectedly. Most of the hands had never met him, and greeted him like they would a dude.

One of the hired help, Jeff, had been given the day off after he helped saddle about eighty horses. He went to the bunkhouse, got a shower and put on his best clothes. He was going into town.

When he came out of the bunkhouse, he did look pretty sharp. He had on a pair of brown jeans, a brown hat, a brown shirt, a matching brown wild rag and polished brown boots. He made quite a sight. He was kinda tall and kinda good-looking at that.

The owner noticed him right away. "Who's that?" he asked.

"That's Jeff," I answered. "He has a day off."

"Does he work here?"

"Yes," I said. "He has the day off," I said again, stressing the fact that Jeff wasn't working. I was hoping the owner wouldn't expect the rest of the hired help to look like that all the time.

"Who hired him?"

"I did," I said. "He's a good hand."

"I can see that! Hum," said the owner, as he looked me over. I was covered in mud, having been in the corral most of the morning catching horses. I thought, as he surveyed my clothing, that he was thinking, *You should have hired him to do your job!*

I felt like telling the owner that, "clothes don't make the man!" but decided to keep my mouth shut.

Nothing more was said and I hoped the owner was satisfied with the business we were doing and the condition of the horses. I knew he didn't like the way most of the hands were covered in mud. It couldn't be helped, and it just came with the territory.

On the same outfit, a high school student we'd hired, Willie, bought a rain suit. It consisted of a rain jacket and pants. Now I don't know if the suit was rubber or plastic. But I do know it was slick! I know that because every time Willie wore his rain suit to keep dry, he came in on foot, his horse having come in before him.

Willie persisted in wearing his rain suit in inclement weather even if it meant he had to walk home! He would come to the stables in his suit, with all the hands watching. After all the comments and snide remarks about his sliding out of the saddle, he would answer, "Yes. But I'm dry!"

Looking for a Job

I always disliked looking for a job. It was time consuming. And a feller always had to fill out job applications, even though I included the same information on my resume. There were a lot of outfits that I'd worked for before and I knew the country, but I had a hankering to see some new country.

I called the brother of a friend of mine in Wyoming and asked him if he knew of anyone looking for help. After a pause, he gave me the name and address of someone in the Jackson, Wyoming, area that might be looking for help.

I made arrangements to drive up and see this individual during the following week.

My son had given me a Pontiac Trans Am and because it got better gas mileage than my truck, I decided to drive it to Jackson. It took about a day to drive to Jackson from where I lived in Colorado and I enjoyed getting good gas mileage. But I didn't enjoy the drive. The seats in the car were uncomfortable and were situated such that my legs and feet were in a more horizontal position than what I was used to. In my truck, my legs and feet were more vertical. In addition, the car had a sunroof and it got awfully hot, even with the air conditioning on. It was a very uncomfortable trip.

I got to Jackson and got a motel room for the night. The next day, I went to apply for a job. When I pulled into the yard, I noticed some hands sitting on the porch drinking coffee.

I parked the car and got out. It was difficult to get out. The car was built low to the ground, and I had to brace myself on the floorboard and crawl out of it, but I managed, after a struggle.

I got out, stretched, and walked to the front porch of the office. I was greeted cordially.

"Come up on the porch and have a cup of coffee," I was told.

I did as instructed. We sat and drank coffee and visited. We spent quite a bit of time visiting and I couldn't see where I was making any progress in getting a job. I was becoming concerned that the job interview was becoming a waste of time and would result without a conclusion or my getting a job.

Finally, I said, "I came up here lookin' for a job and haven't heard anything yet. I don't know if I'm hired or not."

"Oh," said the boss, "you were hired when you got out of the car. We knew you were a cowboy when you walked over here!"

We visited some more and made arrangements for when I would start, as I had to go back to Colorado and take care of some things back there.

I drove back to Colorado, satisfied that I had a job. On the way, I wondered if I really walked like a cowboy or if the position of the seats in the car and the difficulty in getting out of it was what got me hired!

Before I went to work, I gave the car to my daughter. My truck was much more comfortable.

Being a Little Short

Driving a team of horses is fairly easy, particularly if it's a good team that knows its job. One outfit I worked on had a number of teams and each hand was assigned a team to drive for the sleigh rides during the winter.

I didn't much care for the team I drove. The left-hand horse, a bay, I forgot his name, was really sensitive around his ears and bridling him was difficult. I had to undo the cheek strap on the near side, put the snaffle bit in his mouth then fasten the cheek strap. Bridling him was very similar to haltering a horse. The horse was big and I always had to stretch to get the job done. It was always a relief to get him bridled.

The right-hand horse, Big John they called him, had been raised on a bottle and was plumb gentle. He'd been orphaned at a very young age and had been given to the owners of the rental horse stable. He'd had a free run of the whole area while he was on the bottle. He was a light red roan and he turned almost white in the summer.

On one sleigh ride, we encountered a car on our sleigh ride trail. The tourist had pulled off the main road and was trying to use our trail. He didn't get very far until he got stuck. I was following the boss, the second sleigh on this ride.

The boss and his team made it around the stuck car without a problem. The driver of the car was under it, trying to put

cardboard under the tires to get traction. He'd covered himself with a blanket to stay warm while he did this chore.

Big John saw the car, it was on our right, and he'd seen cars before. However, he'd never seen one here. Anything new or out of place can cause a horse to spook and Big John was eyeing the stuck car very suspiciously. As we started around the car, the driver crawled out from under the car with his blanket wrapped loosely around him. He looked just like a bear crawling out from his winter den.

Big John saw this and he wasn't long in trying to get away from this threat! In two jumps he was at a full run. The left-hand horse wasn't long in keeping up with him. I had a runaway!

The boss's granddaughter was riding up front with me and I told her and our other riders to hold on. I couldn't get the team slowed down or stopped.

I tried to turn the team off the trail into the deep snow, but without success. The team had slowed down when they initially saw the stuck car and the boss and his sleigh had got some distance ahead of us about fifty yards. I remember thinking, when I couldn't get the team turned off the trail, "We'll hit that sleigh an' get stopped although it might cause a big wreck."

We were gaining on the lead sleigh fast. My team saw it and slowed down on their own, although I was doing all I could to slow them myself. We didn't hit the lead sleigh.

As we got things under control, I asked our passengers, "Is everybody all right?"

The general consensus was "Yes." Some of our passengers said, "That was fun!"

I just grinned, but didn't agree with them.

I asked the boss's granddaughter, "Are you okay?"

She answered, "Yes. But I was really scared!"

"Me too!" I replied.

The sleigh ride continued without further incident. On the

way home, we had to pass the spot where the car had got stuck. The car was gone, but Big John eyed the area very nervously.

There was another team on this outfit, a nicely matched pair of blacks. They were mostly used in the summer for weddings. Hitched to a big white fancy carriage, they made a very impressive sight.

I'd driven the team of blacks once before and I noticed that the lines on their bridles were kinda short. I made a mental note of this in case I had to drive them again.

We had to use all the teams and sleighs one afternoon. We had a big sleigh ride, a family reunion or something like that. We had to use the blacks.

The boss had hired a new hand a few weeks before and the new hand was selected to drive the blacks. I told him, "The lines are very short, but you'll be all right if you pay attention."

We got everybody loaded in the sleighs. The boss led and the team of blacks followed the boss. My sleigh was third and the boss's brother brought up the tail end behind my sleigh.

The sleigh ride went without incident until we were almost home. We were just walking at a leisurely pace when all of the sudden I saw the team of blacks speed up and turn to the right, off the trail. I couldn't see what spooked them, it was open country.

The driver of the blacks had lost one of the lines, the left one, and had panicked. He was trying to stop the team, but only had one line. Consequently, the more he pulled on the line, the more the team turned to the right. They were off in the deep powder snow and they finally stopped. The riders got off the sleigh and walked to the barn, it was only a hundred yards or so away.

The other sleighs went to the barn and we unloaded our passengers. Then we walked to the team of blacks to see what had happened. The driver had remained with the sleigh.

The boss surveyed the situation. The team was okay, but the tongue to the sleigh was bent at about a 15-degree angle from straight. It took a lot of pressure to bend a two-inch steel pipe to that degree. The boss just shook his head in amazement.

It was a chore to get the sleigh back to the barn, but the team handled it well. The driver didn't handle his being fired so well!

Environmentalist

I'm not really a tree-hugging environmentalist. I guess they have their spot. However, I don't like to see all the garbage I see round the countryside. It's particularly rough around rental horse stables. Anything new or out of place is liable to spook a horse and if the horse doesn't buck the rider off, the rider is liable to fall off if the horse shies or runs off.

And I think it's also particularly disgusting to see cigarette butts and candy wrappers scattered all around the trails.

The plastic sacks that are being used these days are especially dangerous. The wind can blow them quite a ways and when they get caught on the brush and flutter in the wind, it can spook any good horse.

I almost lost my horse one day when we came upon a plastic sack caught on some brush blowing in the wind. I was turned in the saddle, looking back at the dudes I was taking for a ride. My horse saw the sack before I did and immediately spun around and wanted to run back to the corrals. I got him stopped, but not before he was even, head to tail, with the horse behind us. The move was so sudden, I almost fell off!

The horse behind us stopped and didn't move. My horse and I were facing our tourists. I looked back and saw the reason for the horse's fright, a plastic sack fluttering in the wind. I turned and

looked back at the tourists. Some of them had a look of surprise on their faces.

I knew what the situation was now, and simply said to the tourists, "I think my horse just wanted to see what I was lookin' back at."

I got off the horse and led him up to where the sack was. He didn't want to get too close to it. I got the sack from the brush, wadded it up and put it in my pocket. The horse had calmed down. I got back on and rode him past where the sack had been. He was still a little spooked and went around the brush kinda wide, off the trail actually, with his neck arched, ready to run if there was something else there that might hurt him.

Taking care of tourists out on the trail is hard enough, but being a garbage collector at the same time does add some unpleasantness to the job.

Picking the Wrong Horse

I've been considered by some to be a good rider and horseman. I can generally pick a good horse out of a bunch of horses. One day, I was having a real problem and never even got on a horse.

I was at the horse races with an old cowboy friend of mine, Jack Brewer. We were spending an afternoon just watching the races. They had just started to allow betting on the races, they'd never allowed it before, and Jack and I decided to see if we could pick some winners.

I wasn't familiar with the betting system and Jack explained the Win, Place and Show to me. He explained the odds. He told me where to go to place my bet after we'd watched the horses being ponied up and down the track. He also explained the different distances each race was. It was all new to me and I decided to make a bet. Leastways, I figured I could win some just with beginner's luck.

Frankly, for a riding horse, I sorta liked the horses that were leading the race horses better than the race horses themselves! But, before each race, I'd pick the horse I figured would win and made my bet. I didn't pick a winner all day. I couldn't even pick one to Place or Show.

In one race, they led out a really sway-backed older horse. I didn't think he would finish the race, much less run. As it turned out, he won the race by a large margin.

When the sway-backed horse came in first, Jack laughed and said, "I don't think I've ever seen a sway-backed horse that couldn't run!"

"I know why he won that," I said.

"How come?" asked Jack.

"Lookin' at his sway-back and his condition, I figured he thought he had to win or he was going to the glue factory!"

Jack laughed. "You might be right."

All day, I couldn't pick a winner and I got a little discouraged. Jack noticed this and possibly trying to console me, he said, "I think I know why you didn't win anything all day."

"How's that?" I asked.

"It looks like to me that you're picking horses that you would pick to ride on a big circle looking for cattle," said Jack. "These races are only for a hundred yards or a quarter mile or other short distances. You picked some good horses, but not for what they were doing today."

I thought about it and came to the conclusion that Jack was probably right. I also decided that I was not a race horse man!

A Question of Taste

Adam was a good hand. He'd worked for the outfit before but I'd never met him. He was from Arkansas. He showed up a short time after the season started and I'd already showed the new hands the trails, familiarized them with our procedures and done some real basic training for the hands that were pretty green. Adam gave me a hand with the training and I really appreciated it.

I was the barn boss and my boss was Dave, the stable manager. Adam had been the barn boss when he worked for the outfit before, and I was a little concerned about how he would feel about working for me when he'd been the barn boss before. So I asked Dave about it before Adam showed up.

"Adam's a good hand, you should get along well," said Dave.

"I'm a little concerned about how the help will take to takin' orders from two bosses," I said. I continued, "When Steve, the manager on the other side of the mountain, left, there was some confusion as to who was the boss. I got a good deal on supper for all of us at the lodge, and took the whole crew out for a meal. I told them who was boss, let them know what my expectations were and that I could discuss any problems they had after workin' hours. After this supper meeting the crew knew who was boss and what they had to do. We got through the rest of the summer without any problems, although I did get a call from the owner of the outfit later on in the month when he saw the bill for supper. When I explained the situation and circumstances to him, he thought it was a good idea and concurred."

"You won't have any problems with Adam," said Dave.

Dave was right, Adam and I got along well right from the start.

Adam was a good hand with a horse and kinda liked riding the horses that we couldn't rent to the general public. He could take these horses and make more dependable horses of them.

Dave had bought a smaller, young bay mare at the horse sale. It was obvious that this mare had been abused by a previous owner. She was head shy, hard to bridle, in fact she wouldn't even take a bit. She was cinchy and wouldn't stand to be mounted. Dave had told me what he'd paid for the horse and it wasn't much. Watching him trying to get the mare saddled and bridled, I told him, "I can see now why you got her so cheap!"

Our cook, Jeannie, who would rather have been a wrangler—and should have been, she wasn't that good a cook—was watching and took pity on the mare. "I can work her for you," she said.

Jeannie wasn't a good cook and she wasn't much of a horse trainer either. Her horse training came from what she'd read, she'd had very little practical experience training horses. Her policy seemed to be based on love, tolerance, kindliness, and patience. Of these four items, patience is the most important. Horses learn by repetition, doing the same thing the same way over and over. Love is nice, but doesn't teach the horse anything. And love of what you're doing when you're training a horse is important. But love of a horse just because he's a horse and he's a big and beautiful horse doesn't accomplish anything for the horse.

Tolerance is important, but it's important to remember not to tolerate poor or bad behavior. In a herd of horses, they don't tolerate bad behavior and the punishment for such behavior is swift and quite harsh. Kindliness is nice, but if a horse is treated kindly, there's no harm done, unless the horse is treated real kindly with,

say, a sugar cube, it won't be long before the kindliness is repaid with a shirt ripped off by the horse.

Jeannie was so loving, kind, tolerant and patient with this mare that it wasn't long before she couldn't get the mare to leave the yard, unless she followed another horse. And it was becoming more of a problem. I'd noticed this, but didn't say anything. Dave noticed it also and finally told Adam to take the horse and tune her up.

Adam put his saddle on the mare and started to work her. He wasn't abusive, although the untrained eye might think he was pretty rough. However, he was making the horse do what he wanted her to do.

Jeannie was watching but didn't say anything. She later made the comment that "Adam ruined the horse!"

At the risk of getting lousier cooking, I came to Adam's defense when I told her, "You let the mare get away with everythin' and she got to the point where you couldn't even ride her out on the trail. Adam got her to payin' attention an' doin' what he wanted her to do. He simply got firm with her."

Jeannie didn't have an answer for that, but I noticed that Jeannie didn't take out as many rides as she had in the past. And the rides she went on, she didn't lead, she followed. The mare would follow out of the yard.

The summer wore on and the mare got rode less and less, and the cooking didn't get any better. The afternoon rainstorms came on a regular basis and the corrals became a mess of manure and mud. It got real slick out in the corrals and it was difficult to stay upright if a feller had to move fast.

We were sorting horses one afternoon and Adam lost his footing. He went down face first. When he got up, he was covered from his feet to the top of his head with a mixture of mud and manure. As he carefully wiped the dirt from his eyes, nose and mouth, he said, "So that's what that tastes like!"

"Adam," I said, "you've tasted that before. You already knew what it tasted like."

"Well," replied Adam, "it's been a long time. So long in fact, that I was beginning to wonder if I was tasting it at every meal!"

Adam didn't think much of the cooking either.

Repeat Performance

When I was younger, a teenager, I figured myself to be a pretty good bronc rider. I actually had thoughts of being a top-notch saddle bronc rider in the rodeos. I had daydreams about winning all the major rodeos in the saddle bronc riding. I was getting some practice on a few colts we had at the ranch—they'd buck a little. I managed to stay on them most of the time and I tended to overestimate my abilities on bucking horses.

When a colt bogged his head and started to buck, I encouraged him, certain that I could ride him and eventually he'd tire of this activity and quit. When he'd done this activity enough and found he couldn't throw me, he'd quit for good. Yep, I figured myself to be a good horse breaker and bronc rider.

One of the hands noticed that I was encouraging these colts to buck when they started and he told me, "You'll do a better job of breakin' these colts if you don't let them buck."

"But that would take all the fun out of it," I retorted.

"You keep doin' that an' you'll find that some of 'em like to buck, then you'll have your hands full. They'll buck every time you saddle 'em. Then they'll never be considered broke completely. They'll never become trustworthy."

"I can ride 'em enough that they'll come around," I said.

These colts were two-year-olds and hadn't fully developed. What little riding I was doing on them wouldn't hurt them at all and would help them develop their muscles. I figured I was helping them and they were helping me develop my bronc riding skills. As two-year-olds, they didn't buck very hard, but I was getting some practice.

One day, a new horse showed up at the ranch. He was owned by the neighbors and they were having a hard time breaking him.

"We heard that you had a good bronc rider over here." I immediately felt the pride building up when I heard that. "This horse has been started," the neighbor continued, "but he's bad to buck. He's thrown me a number of times and I'm getting too old to take it. Maybe you can take the buck out of him."

Confidant that I could manage, I said, "I'll bet we can."

I looked the horse over. He was about four years old and was well developed. He was big and stout. I didn't anticipate any unusual problems as I got my saddle on him. He'd been started and

had good ground manners and I didn't have any problems. I figured the horse had the neighbor buffaloed.

I untracked the horse, checked the cinch and climbed on him. I sat there for a minute and rocked the saddle back and forth sideways with no response from the horse. I touched him with a spur and he broke loose. He bogged his head and went to bucking and he knew how to buck!

He loosened me on the first jump, ducked to the side on the second jump and bucked me off on the third jump. I hit the ground and immediately got up. I thought to myself, *He has no right to dump me like that, the good bronc rider that I am!*

The horse just stood in the corral and watched me. He had a look on his face that seemed to say, "That wasn't so tough. Want to try me again?"

Of course I had to get on again and we went through the same procedure again, with the same results. All in all, that horse bucked me off five times that day!

Finally, the hand that had told me that some of the colts might learn to like bucking, said, "Better call it a day. You keep gettin' off that horse that way, you'll ruin him!"

Jealousy

When I was a kid, about fifteen or sixteen—it's been quite a few years, I can't remember exactly—I was working during the summer vacation from school for a sheep rancher in eastern Utah. During the first part of June we'd spend the mornings docking lambs. It was a dirty job and the sheep rancher was one of the largest in the state. He also had about a hundred head of cows.

My job was to hold the lambs on a bench while one of the older hands did the docking and castrating. It was dirty because when the tails of the lambs were cut off, the man doing the docking would push the tail up against the stomach of the lamb, thereby sending a stream of blood from the docked tail all over the holder—me. It was wise not to wear clean clothes for this operation.

When all the lambs had been docked, earmarked, and branded with paint, the morning's work was done and we'd go back to the main ranch to get cleaned up and have our noon meal.

After eating, I'd generally saddle a horse, load him in a truck and go out and look for lost sheep or look after his cows. I did have a colt or two to ride. I'd generally go in the area where the herd we'd just docked had been. The owner had a list of the numbers of sheep in each herd and if there were a few missing sheep from that herd, I'd go look for them.

One day, I didn't have to go looking for lost sheep. I was selected to help the owner's oldest son deliver supplies to some of

FR. LOREN SCHMIDT

the sheepherders farther away from the main ranch. It wasn't hard work and I got a chance to see some country I hadn't seen before.

At one sheep camp there was an old Mexican sheepherder. He didn't speak English but the owner's son was fluent in Spanish. I looked the old herder over and could tell he was an old cowboy. His chaps were well worn, showing signs of being used in the saddle many years. He had the typical walk of a long time horseman.

I unloaded his supplies while the owner's son talked with him. I don't speak Spanish but did pick up a few words that I knew. I saw a look of surprise come over the old herder's face when I heard the owner's son say, "Aqui es mi vaquero." The old herder had a look of disbelief on his face.

On the way back to the ranch, the owner's son told me what he had said to the herder and we both had a good laugh over it.

The following week was spent in the same routine as the previous weeks—docking lambs in the morning and hunting lost sheep or moving cattle in the afternoon.

One day, the owner's son came to me after we were done docking lambs and said, "One of our herders quit this morning."

"Really?" I replied. "Which one?"

"Do you remember the old herder that I told that you were my cowboy?"

"Yep," I answered.

"Well, that's the one. I gave him a ride out to the highway."

"Why did he quit?" I asked.

"Apparently he thought you were too young to be a good cowboy and he thought he ought to have the job."

"That's too bad," I said, hoping that I wouldn't be selected to replace him. "What are you going to do?"

"We'll find another herder. That's the first time I had a herder quit because of jealousy."

"Jealousy?" I asked.

"Yes. He wanted your job!"

Skunk

Skunk was an old mare when we got her. She was a bay mare with a lot of white spots running down her back. She was gentle and slow. Slow isn't always bad, especially in a dude operation. At our horse rental business, prior riding experience isn't required to ride on our guided rides and enjoy the scenery, wildlife and experience.

Even though prior riding experience isn't required to ride with us, when assigning horses to customers, we always asked, "How much have you ridden before?"

Answers would vary from "None" to "I'm an experienced rider." Quite often, with the so-called experienced riders, we'd give them a slower horse. People tend to overestimate their horsemanship skills and we didn't want any jackpots occurring out on the trail.

Skunk was a kid's horse. She just carried kids over six and weighing up to about eighty pounds. At her age, I didn't want to use her too hard. She only had a few years left, but she did have to pay her own way.

One day we had a peculiar problem. A lady showed up with her grandson and he had some special needs. We weren't a therapeutic riding center. Therapeutic riding centers have special equipment and plenty of help to lead the horse and side walkers to assist the rider.

The grandmother told me that her grandson was autistic, but had ridden a lot before.

After explaining our situation to the grandmother, I told her, "I'm really reluctant to take the youngster out on the trail for safety reasons. We don't have the equipment or personnel to keep not only your grandson safe, but everyone else on the ride safe."

However, Grandma was insistent. At the risk of a court case regarding equal opportunity for the disabled, I relented.

Although Skunk had already been used for an hour ride earlier in the day, I called one of the hands to bring her out. Trying to limit her work load, we only generally used her once a day. However, she would be the perfect horse for this autistic youngster.

We had an alley, about twelve feet wide, where we put people on their horses. When everyone was horseback, we gave instructions and then rode the corral area, single file.

Skunk and her rider followed everyone out of the alley. As soon as Skunk got clear of the alley, the youngster gave her a couple of hard kicks in the ribs and Skunk took off as fast as she could go!

I was watching and was surprised. Skunk showed more life than I thought she had. Some of the other horses shied in surprise as Skunk passed them, but fortunately, nobody fell off.

Everyone, including myself, was yelling at the youngster, "Pull back on the reins! Pull back on the reins!"

However, the autistic youngster ignored our requests. He seemed to be enjoying his adventure. I was worried that he would fall off.

One of our more experienced hands, an outrider on this ride, told the riders, "Stay here! I'll catch him!"

Rather than taking off behind Skunk, the rider made a big circle around her and managed to stop her. Skunk was more than willing to stop! The hand made a circle around Skunk because if a person tries to catch a runaway horse by following directly behind, the affair becomes a horse race.

The outrider led Skunk back to the other riders. I was still at the stables, not able to go on the ride. Someone had to watch the office.

I told the outrider, "You better lead this youngster on the rest of the ride. We don't need any more excitement today!"

The ride continued, safely. The grandma told me later that, "He's only ridden at a therapeutic riding center in the corral. This is his first time outside the corral."

Other Books by Stu Campbell

Horsing Around a Lot

Horsing Around the Dudes

Humor Around Horses

You Can't Be Serious!

Comedy Around the Corral

More Humor Around Horses

Muddy Waters

A Young Cowboy's Adventure Series

A Young Cowboy's Adventure
Honey
Surprise!
Intruders
Expectations
Frozen
Advice
Broken
Ginny

Wild Horses for Wild Kids
The Kids Get Horses

About the Artist

True Cowboy Artist, R. Loren Schmidt, continues to this day to ride horses and work cattle. The cowboy life is what inspires his artwork. His models are good friends and genuine working cowboys. All of Loren's illustrations are drawn from real life experiences. This is the sixth book he has illustrated for his friend of twenty years, Stu Campbell.